I Love You, Mr. Melon Bear

It was a cold February day in Shadowy Hollow.

"Ready to go celebrate Valentine's Day with Mr. Melon Bear?" asked Marie.

"Yep, and I got all the stuff," Stevie agreed.

After a little walking, Stevie said, "I don't recognize any of this."

"Yeah, the forest looks different. How will we find Mr. Melon Bear?"

"Hello," called a voice.

"Oh, hello," said Marie, spotting a robin just above them.

"Are you looking for Mr. Melon Bear?"

"Yes, it's hard to tell which way to go. Where is everyone?"

"Well, all animals are hibernating."

"What's hibernating?" asked Stevie.

"It's when animals like your friend Mr. Melon Bear find a cozy den to sleep and stay warm during the cold winter months."

"What about you?"

"We robins fly south for the winter. This is warmer than my home."

"Wow, we just learned something new," Marie confessed.

"Ms. Robin, could you take us to Mr. Melon Bear's den?"

"Absolutely. Follow me," replied Ms. Robin.

The children followed her through the wintry forest.

As she ran, Marie dropped candies down on the snow for an easy way back.

The children found a large hole dug into the hill.
They could barely make out the familiar brown—furred
creature snoring inside. "Is it Mr. Melon Bear?"
"Yep, and he snores louder than dad!" Marie laughed.

The children excitedly knocked all around Mr. Melon Bear's den, but no matter how much they banged, he wouldn't wake.

"I have an idea," said Marie.

She quickly pulled a thermos from her backpack.

"With his strong sense of smell, I bet this cider will wake him."

Suddenly, Mr. Melon Bear began to rise.

With his eyes still shut, Mr. Melon Bear inched forward until he bumped his nose right into the thermos.

"Careful," Stevie giggled.

"Stevie?" said Mr. Melon Bear groggily.

Mr. Melon Bear opened his eyes as wide as he could
and saw the children standing before him. "Kids!" he exclaimed.
The children laughed as they squeezed him back.

It's so good to see you, but why are you here?

It's freezing outside!" Mr. Melon Bear asked.

"We're here to celebrate Valentine's Day with you!"

Mr. Melon Bear seemed confused. "What's Valentine's Day?"

Stevie and Marie looked at each other in disbelief.

How could Mr. Melon Bear not know about Valentine's Day?

"Valentine's Day is a day to celebrate love," Marie explained.

"There are all different kinds of love," chimed Stevie.

"I love watermelon," said Mr. Melon Bear.

"Loving delicious food is a kind of love,
but different than the ones we're talking about," continued Marie.
"When you love someone, it's more special and unique."

"I love Stevie because he's my brother.

We do almost everything together.

That's family love.

Mom and Dad loved each other so much

they got married and had us.

That's romantic love."

"The last major kind of love is friendship.
Friends are people you share special times with,
but who may not always be around," finished Marie.

I think about the fun I have with you all the time,

and I care very much about you, so that means

the love we have is friendship!" Mr. Melon Bear exclaimed.

"Aww, Mr. Melon Bear," gushed Marie.

"We love you too," confessed Stevie.

"So how do we celebrate our friendship
on Valentine's Day?" asked Mr. Melon Bear.

"Usually everything is red with hearts and sometimes flowers," described Marie.

"And there's candy," added Stevie, "usually in heart boxes."

"That sounds exciting," said Mr. Melon Bear,

"but I don't have any of that."

"Let's go for a walk and see what we can find," said Marie. When they stepped outside, Mr. Melon Bear spotted something mysterious hanging from a tree branch.

"What's this?" asked Mr. Melon Bear.

"It looks like a Valentine's Day note," said Stevie.

"But who would've left it?" wondered Mr. Melon Bear.

"Let's find out," urged Marie.

Mr. Melon Bear read the note: "*Follow the candy back.*"

"Maybe it's follow the candy back...

to a Valentine's Day surprise!" said Marie.

"A new mystery to solve together," declared Mr. Melon Bear

The three friends took off to look for candy

until they arrived at a familiar spot not far from camp.

"I don't see any more candies," said Mr. Melon Bear.

"Look! There's an envelope on that branch!" Marie yelled out.

Mr. Melon Bear tried to reach the envelope,

but it suddenly flew away. They all ran after it,

but it flew further and further away.

Luckily, Ms. Robin was flying by, and she grabbed the envelope. Inside there was a card.

To: Mr. Melon Bear
Roses are red,
Violets are blue,
Happy Valentine's Day
from us to you!

♡Marie and Stevie

LOVE

"It was you kids all along?"

"Yep, and we brought you this," said Stevie.

"Watermelon, my favorite! But I don't have anything for you."

"Celebrating our friendship together is all we need," said Marie, smiling.

"Well, at least I can share this watermelon with you.

Anybody else hungry?"

"I'm starved," confessed Stevie.

"Sounds great," agreed Marie.

THE END

Made in United States
North Haven, CT
03 February 2022

15602568R00020